# THE GIANT'S CHILD

### AND OTHER STORIES

John McInnes, *Senior Author*

John Ryckman

**NELSON** CANADA

© Nelson Canada,
A Division of International Thomson Limited, 1987

Published in 1987 by
Nelson Canada,
A Division of International Thomson Limited
1120 Birchmount Road
Scarborough, Ontario
M1K 5G4

ISBN 0-17-602474-3

**Canadian Cataloguing in Publication Data**

McInnes, John, 1927-
   The Giant's Child and Other Stories

(Networks)

ISBN 0-17-602474-3

1. Readers (Primary). I. Ryckman, John, 1928-
II. Title. III. Series: Networks (Toronto, Ont.)

PE1119.M2537 1987    428.6    C86-093636-8

Printed and bound in Canada

# Contents

# I Hate Peas!

I hate peas!
They are small and green
and roll around my plate.
They shoot all over the table.
I can never catch them with my fork.
I hate everything about peas!

My friend Jason loves peas!
He spears them with his fork
and pops them into his mouth.
Jason loves everything about peas!

My friend Jason hates spaghetti!
It is long and white
and slops around on his plate.
It slips off his fork
and slithers off his chin.
Jason hates everything about spaghetti!

I love spaghetti!
I wind it around my fork
and slide it into my mouth.
I love everything about spaghetti!

I hate mashed potatoes!
They are mushy and white
and they bury my carrots.
They steal my gravy
and stick to my fork.
I hate everything about mashed potatoes!

My friend Jason loves mashed potatoes!
He makes them into mountains
and roads and ponds.
Jason loves everything about mashed potatoes!

I love peanut butter!
It is thick and crunchy
and it always sticks where I put it.
I love everything about peanut butter!

Jason loves peanut butter, too!
He likes everything about peanut butter.
So when Jason comes to my house,
guess what we have to eat!

# All the Animals Were Angry

*by William Wondriska*

It was a hot day in the jungle. The animals had nothing to do.

The lion was angry. He walked over to the turtle and said, "I hate you because you're so slow."

The turtle was angry. He looked up at the elephant and said, "I hate you because you're so big."

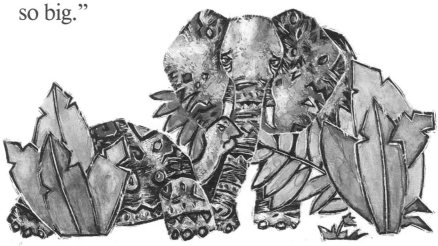

The elephant was angry. He looked down at the ant and said, "I hate you because you're so small."

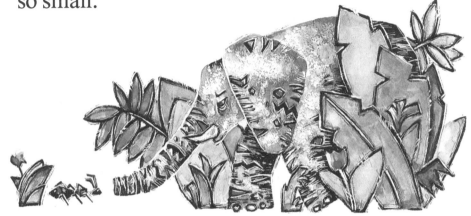

The ant was angry. He looked up at the giraffe and said, "I hate you because you're so tall."

The giraffe was angry. He looked at the snake and said, "I hate you because you're so quiet."

The snake was furious. He looked up at the lion and said, "I hate you because you're so loud."

All the animals were so angry they were ready to tear each other to pieces.

Suddenly a dove flew down from the sky. He looked at the lion and with a happy face said, "I love you because sometimes it's good to be loud."

The lion looked happy. "You do?" he asked.

The dove flew to the turtle and said, "I love you because sometimes it's good to be slow."

The turtle looked happy. "You do?" he asked.

The dove flew to the elephant and said, "I love you because sometimes it's good to be big."

The elephant looked happy. "You do?" he asked.

The dove flew to the ant and said, "I love you because sometimes it's good to be small."

The ant looked happy. "You do?" he asked.

The dove flew over to the giraffe and said, "I love you because sometimes it's good to be tall."

The giraffe looked happy. "You do?" he asked.

The dove flew to the snake and said, "I love you because sometimes it's good to be quiet."

The snake looked happy. "You do?" he asked.

"Yes, I do," replied the dove. "I love you all."

It was a hot day in the jungle. The animals still had nothing to do. But, they were happy.

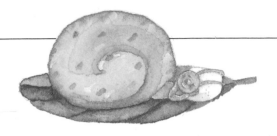

# The Giant's Child

## Part One: In the Garden

Every morning, when the first rays of sunlight touched her pillow, the giant's child would open her eyes, stretch her arms, wiggle her toes, and say to herself, "Today is going to be a wonderful day." Then the giant's child would jump out of bed, get dressed, eat her breakfast, and run outside to play in the garden.

The giant's child had a beautiful garden. Flowers grew everywhere. Birds sang in the trees. Fountains splashed and sparkled in the sunlight.

The giant's child would play in her garden all day long. At the end of the day, she would say to herself, "I will never, ever leave my garden."

One morning, when the giant's child was playing in her garden, she heard someone crying. She looked over the wall and saw a small boy clinging to a branch of a tree.

The giant's child reached over the wall. Very carefully, she lifted the small boy down from the tree. The small boy looked up at the giant's child. Then, without a word, he turned and ran away.

Later that same day, the giant's child was watching some birds playing in her fountain. A big splash startled her. A ball had landed in the water.

The giant's child looked over the wall. She saw the same small boy muttering to himself.

The giant's child picked up the ball and tossed it to the boy. He looked at the giant's child and smiled. Then he turned and ran away.

The next day, when the giant's child was playing in her garden, she heard someone calling, "Help! Help!" The giant's child looked over the wall. It was the same small boy.

"Help!" he called. "Please help! My friends are out on the lake and can't get back to shore."

The giant's child climbed over the wall and hurried down to the lake. She waded out to the boat. Very carefully, she towed the boat back to shore.

The children looked up at the giant's child. "Thanks!" they shouted. Then they all turned and ran away.

At the end of the day, the giant's child looked at her garden. "Everything is beautiful," she said. "I would be very happy if I never, ever left my garden. But outside my garden, there are children who need my help. Tomorrow I'll go and look for them."

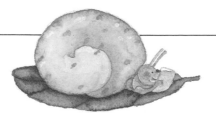

## Part Two: Over the Wall

The next morning, the giant's child hurried outside to her garden. She smelled the flowers, listened to the birds, and watched the fountains splashing and sparkling in the sunlight. Then the giant's child climbed over the wall.

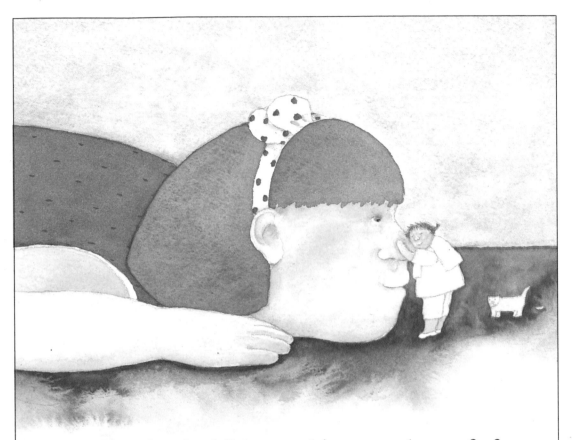

The giant's child saw a kitten on the roof of a house. A little girl was calling to the kitten. She was holding up a saucer of milk.

Very carefully, the giant's child lifted the kitten from the roof and set it on the ground.

"You saved my kitten!" cried the little girl. Then she gave the giant's child a hug.

The giant's child saw some children with a baby bird. It had fallen out of its nest. The children were trying to help the baby bird back to its nest.

Very carefully, the giant's child picked up the baby bird and put it back in the nest.

"It's good that you're so tall!" laughed one of the children.

The giant's child saw smoke billowing into the sky. It was coming from a burning roof. Some children were running away from it. They were calling, "Fire! Fire!"

The giant's child hurried to the lake. She scooped up some water in her hands and threw it on the roof. Soon, the fire was out.

A boy called out, "Hurrah! Hurrah for the giant's child!"

All the children danced around the giant's child and shouted, "Hurrah!"

The giant's child smiled at the children. Then she waved goodbye and headed for home.

*Project Manager*: Christine Anderson
*Senior Editor*: Jocelyn Van Huyse
*Series Design*: Rob McPhail and Lorraine Tuson
*Design and Art Direction*: Lorraine Tuson
*Cover Design*: Taylor/Levkoe Associates Limited
*Cover Illustration*: Mireille Levert
*Typesetting*: Trigraph Inc.
*Printing*: Friesen Printers

**Acknowledgements**

All selections in this book were written or adapted by John McInnes and John Ryckman, with the exception of the following:

*All the Animals Were Angry* by William Wondriska: Copyright © 1970 by William Wondriska. Reprinted by permission of Henry Holt and Company, Inc.

**Illustrations**

Philippe Béha: 4-9
Mireille Levert: 20-31
Lorraine Tuson: 10-19

6 7 8 9 0 FP 2 1 0